The Woman Out of Now

"And we who are we anyhow"
- Plotinus

Biagi

Biagi Books are available for order
through Ingram Press Catalogues

This book is a work of fiction. Names, characters, places,
and incidents either are products of the author's imagination
or are used fictitiously. Any resemblance to actual persons,
living or dead, events, or locales is entirely coincidental.

Biagi
Visit my website at www.----------------

Printed in the United States of America
First Printing: December 2014
Published by Sojourn Publishing, LLC

ISBN: 978-1-62747-102-2
Ebook ISBN: 978-1-62747-103-9
LCN: Pending

Table of Contents

Acknowledgement

All my thanks to Tom Bird, RamaJon and all the other members of Sojourn Publishing without whose help this book would never have been written or published.

Sleepstirring song wakes, pulls,
stretching through realms
from the one place.
Sleepstirring song untangles the wave dreams
we are.
Calls,
stretching through realms
from the one place.

Our song, the dream song,
we,
break free,
drifting ebb and flow,
through the many,
seeping foamwedded, pulsedrawn,
slipping through surfaces,
entering and leaving.

Sleepstirring song calls forth
Membrance
of how we come from the one place

Each song, recalls the first song.

Chapter One

T his is the beginning and also the end. For a beginning is also an end. There comes an image, an image that haunts me awake and dreaming. It covers my walls with the deep vibrancy of its rainbow colors. I will not rest or sleep peacefully until I bring it to life. It beckons to me in my restless dreams, in the deep purple darkness of the night, through the black, silent emptiness of my inner self, through the quiet promise of a brilliant dawn, a golden dawn of mind, of body, of spirit. It is the beginning.

Night after persistent night the ghostly image appears, a pearly, translucent painting covering the wall across from my bed. It starts out as an intimidating, shining blank white space and through the night grows rich and detailed. Golden, cloud like mist and iridescent blue, red and green shapes take form mixing, twisting and wrapping around each other. At times the mist parts opening into an infinite golden emptiness. Shadowy figures float in and out of the space looming and fading invitingly into the distance. And then the shifting colors reflected in the pearly essence lift majestically from the image and drift sensuously towards me, covering me, entering me with its body warmth, its deep body taste and its blossoming, musky perfume. The softest silk caresses me with the gentle wind of a first spring day, resonating its rhythm into my every living cell. And in its midst I feel the sensuous presence of breasts, hips and thighs. I feel caressing arms insistently pulling me into the soft, yielding warmth. I taste the salty ripeness of lips and tongue pressed against my face, my lips, entering my mouth, an inviting, seductive presence that embraces and enfolds me. Each night the mist becomes denser, more demanding, holding me passionately within its intimate embrace.

Morning after empty, hollow morning I reluctantly wake. I wake to no image, no golden hued passionate goddess. Only a blank grey wall remains and so I try fruitlessly to recreate my dream image but it doesn't come. I desperately struggle night after disappointing night yearning for the ghostly presence that gloriously haunts my dreams. Night after lonely night I paint, throwing a mélange of colors onto the wall, hoping that they will miraculously collect into the magic of the misty image, calling for the warm embrace of a golden goddess. I yearn for more than this ghostly being. I want to see and feel the realness of her face, feel the waking, temptation of her body. I long to know she is more than a glorious, beautiful dream. But the warm sensuous presence visits only in my dreams, only in my deepest sleep. Night after night I work feverishly until I collapse exhausted onto the bed.

And again each night I dream; the golden transforming presence, the image I must paint, that visits in the night, the presence who embraces me in the night. Until finally, until finally I see a perfectly beautiful angelic face close to mine as her body presses against me. Then in the midst of one magical night, I awake, I believe I am awake, I don't know, I fully embrace a soft enticing woman stretched beside me. Her tender lips search for mine in the dark and then she slowly turns into the soft pulsating mist and majestically drifts back into the painting.

I reach desperately for her, my finger passing helplessly through the mist as she drifts away, leaving me with the deep emptiness of an unformed being. As I frantically look into the glowing image a figure slowly emerges, a ghostly, almost transparent woman, until finally a mist lifts from the image and moves toward me. It condenses and solidifies and the luscious body of this glorious woman covers me, presses into me.

I drift into a questioning wakefulness. At least I believe I wake and see the image-the transforming image. The glowing, pulsating image resonates through my inner core transforming every sense of myself, an image I sense will transform the world, what has come to me in the stillness of the night. And as I look,

I see forms shift and change, moving into new intricate patterns that somehow reach into me and unstring me. The golden mist majestically lifts from the painting and as in the dream drifts towards me, pulsating and condensing and finally a form emerges into the perfect fullness of the woman.

Mists wrap and swirl around her, a magic gossamer garment. Her angelic face appears in the changing forms. Her raven hair and dark eyes contrast the golden mist and the golden hue of her skin. She is a striking study of dark and gold framed in a slender, almost angelic form. The mist parts and then reforms and parts to reveal her. Her body has the same ephemeral quality of the mist yet carries all the sensual quality of ideal womanly beauty, the beauty that is part of every woman, the ideal that manifests every sense of what beauty is.

I recognize that face, the face that has appeared in all of my dreams, that now touches and kisses me, the mysterious face that I have seen only in the long still nights and yet is familiar, a mysterious entity, a being from another world or time or dimension. I don't know. And yet the face is so familiar. Someone

I might have known in another time and place, another world, someone who did not enter this existence with me and yet is always close. A mysterious being far removed from this existence has come to me, for what purpose I don't know, and yet I feel through every fiber of my being she brings the beginning.

The mist enfolds me touching every surface of my skin with a vibrating, tingling sensation. It enters my ears, nose, mouth, every opening in my body. Am I being possessed? But no, I have never felt more myself. My sense of who I am and what I must be intensifies and magnifies. I feel a glorious love seep through me filling me with the sense of my deepest self, my most true glorious self.

Her musky perfume promises every heavenly pleasure. Her soft, full lips move close to my ear. She has the insubstantiality of mist but I can feel every part of her body as she holds me. We stand entwined in a close, passionate embrace and then she speaks. Her voice carries all the vibrations of a heavenly chorus. "Find me," she sings. As I hold her I feel her body become more substantial I feel whatever spirit she is becoming more physical, and then she lifts away from me and dissolves into the mist, into the painting.

Am I truly awake or still dreaming, but whether I am awake or dreaming I know I must begin. I must begin the search.

Chapter Two

I leave walking out into the cold, damp night-searching, stepping over the sleeping bodies of homeless men. Broken men used up and no longer useful, thrown by the regime out of the compounds into the streets. I hurry through the stench of unwashed, sick and rotting bodies. Deep sadness and helplessness twist my heart in the face of a heartless regime that treats these men as nothing more than human refuse.

I walk aimlessly. Searching for that one face. Why is it familiar, where could I have seen it?

There are lost others milling about –the usual street girls waiting to entrap sex seeking men. I pass them by, knowing the danger, knowing that if I go with them I will vanish. I will disappear into the dark, deserted looking buildings.

I walk and walk, long into the night - seeing the faces - the desperate empty faces and empty eyes and I look for hope and beauty and mostly love. I look for the hope and love I saw in her face, in the image, where is she? Where would she be? What draws me to the streets? Why do I think she could be in the streets? Yet I keep walking and searching.

Women beckon, and speak to me. Someone stops me. She grabs me, pressing her body hard against me, and promises a night of exquisite pleasure. Her drawn face betrays her desperation, the lost, drugged look in her eyes. She is one of them, girls and boys, sent by the regime out into the night to lure lonely, desperate men into the buildings.

I remember the dire warnings. The exquisite pleasure she promises lays waiting in one of the windowless building where they will tie me down to a table and insert tubes into my body to extract sperm. This will continue as long I last, as long as I produce.

Women who don't cooperate with the regime or who do not meet their quota of luring sperm producers end up in the same buildings where the regime straps them to a table. The faceless technicians mechanically insert sperm into them until they become pregnant. The regime holds them for as long as they can become pregnant and bear babies. It discards the bodies of both men and women once they are no longer useful, dumping them outside the compounds where there is no food, no means to survive. The puritanical regime tyrannically and harshly punishes any sexual encounter or advance.

Many of us feed and comfort the broken bodies, but so many are lost both in body and mind. The few we save join us, the others we comfort and make their passing as comfortable as possible.

Indoctrination technicians raise the offspring in incubation facilities and then send most of the teens to factories and farms where they work the rest of their lives to produce food and other goods for the corporations and rulers of the regime. They draft others as soldiers. And thus the puritanical regime replenishes itself. It bans normal child bearing along with any sexual activity.

I beware of the trappings of sex and any kind of attraction.

In spite of my fear and trepidation I continue my desperate search through the streets. Is she one of the sirens luring me to my doom? I am afraid but keep walking. Where will she appear? And then long into the night I see her. A woman stands on a street corner, the one I have been looking for. I have seen her before on the same corner. She appears different from the others and carries a lost and bewildered air as though she has found herself there with no idea of how she got there. I have never seen her with other men but she often stands alone as though looking for something or someone and in spite of my attraction I have been too afraid to approach her. But I have watched her through many nights and tried to follow her. I have never seen her come out of the dark buildings or the compound. I have never seen where she goes as the night ends. Often I would look and suddenly see her standing in a doorway or on a corner and just as suddenly she would disappear into some deep darkness.

But now her body is covered in a robe that drifts and moves sometimes covering her figure, sometime revealing it. A glow emanates from her, a soft warm glow that draws me to her. Her face now is the face that comes to me in the night. I realize that she resembles the golden woman but now through some magical transformation she has become that woman. She moves toward me and looks into my eyes, drawing me closer. She is the one. Her eyes fill me with wonder; fill me with joy, but also with a deep longing.

She speaks, a soft melody, and her voice resonates through me. It tangles itself in my being. The sensual rich quality of her voice enthralls me. I cannot place it. It has a sense of the lost within it, of a lost world, of insubstantiality. She is not yet real. Something dreamlike emanates from her, as though she is not completely here with me, as though she is possessed, as though the woman who visits me in my dreams has to find her and inhabit her as her physical self, has to take hold of her physical being.

She does not fully belong to this world. She remains part image, part woman. I feel as though she has just appeared out of the mist of the image and has just become fully human and accommodated to our world.

This is why I had to search for her. She needed me to find the person who is the outward manifestation of the woman in the mist.

She appears the same as the other street girls, but I sense the difference. Her body gives off a different perfume, the essence of all the blossoms that could ever possibly exist. It both seduces and reaches deeper into some memory within me, a memory of a lost land, a lost self.

I try to speak, but nothing comes. And then she takes my arm and we walk, not into the darkened buildings where they wait for us, but to my home, the place where I live and work in the secrecy of the night and I am not afraid. She stops in front of the image and turns her face towards me in the golden light, the same light she radiates and walks into the image.

I desperately search the image looking for some hint of her presence but she has again become part of the shapes, part of the mist. Will she return?

I drop into my bed exhausted and wondering- to see her absorbed by the colors, the mist, to lose her among the forms and see her transform again into an image. I wonder why? Why did I have to search for her out in the night? Was it a test? And then I realize that she needed to find her place in this world, to be sure that she belongs here, to find her physical self. She needed to join her purely conscious self with her physical self. She comes for a reason and needs to know she belongs here, that this is the place.

Chapter Three

A gain I fall into a deep sleep and dream long into the night. I dream of her, of the painting, of her face, of her touch, and of her return. I dream of painting into the image, of that other world, that other place, where she comes from, a world so different from ours, and yet so present, folded into our space. It lies so close under the surface touching all the possibilities of our existence, showing us a world that could be, holding all the promise of what we can be. It gives birth to us, the place we enter from, where we have existed through all space and time, the place we travel from into our world. I almost see it; I almost touch its texture. I hear its heavenly music, a chorus of angelic voices inspiring what I paint. I smell the ambrosia of its intimate presence. It waits for us to make it happen, for our world to open into it. The brush takes control and brings that world onto the wall. In the dream I understand.

But when I wake it fades. Every dreaming thought, everything I knew, the feeling, every intuition vanishes. I reach for it, try to grasp it, but it slips into the emptiness, the mysterious place beyond the understanding of my waking mind. I begin painting feverishly, hoping an answer will come.

What mystical being has come to us? Where does she come from? Where does she go? Time passes and I deliriously paint. The image shifts. I sense her presence but in an almost unreachable different form. What magic brings her to us? In the yearning of my heart I know she will return.

The layers shift in the image-layers of time? Shifting from one level to another-are they the future, the past? I know they contain both, all the layers of time, in the now. My consciousness shifts recognizing the truth, recognizing that past and future are now. They belong to this world and yet are not here. They bring a hope, a dream, of what we can be- a new beginning. They open a door into richer, deeper reality, an opening into that magical world that lies beyond.

The mists flow forming and reforming and out of the opening a radiant figure materializes. She steps again into our world.

"The time has finally come," she says, "the time to truly awaken and to awaken the world. We are the new beings and we are the ancient watchers. All of time reaches us here in the now." She takes my hand. She leads me into the image. I feel the warmth of her touch seeping through me. I see the passion in her eyes. Her eyes contain all the layers of being- the eternal mists shifting from beneath, and together we enter the other existence. The world that touches ours and brings what should be. We enter the image, enter the emptiness, and pass through into a new light.

Chapter Four

We fly. She guides me into an ecstatic dance, moving with the ever changing mist, feeling the deep pulses and rhythms of a primal resonant music, leaping joyously from cloud to cloud. I have never felt such joy, such exaltation. I have never felt such power and moved with such grace and agility. This is who I truly am; this is the essence of my truest self. I have awakened to my primal being, the self who carries all the love and wisdom of the creative source.

Others approach, others who join in the dance. Smiling, happy, beguiling figures, shadows that float in and out of focus. She leads me into awakening realms. The wonder of it seizes me. Is this the imaginings of my deepest, dreamlike desires or have I truly awakened and entered all the dimensions of existence?

She sings and her voice touches all the longing in my heart. She sings of something beyond all language, something outside our world, from a place that knows no limitations in space or time.

She sings of being, of the Source, beyond all mind and matter, of our immense journey through all the universes, of our entry into this universe. Of two streams, the conscious and the physical, and how they enter this universe as it blossoms from the Source, the tree of all universes.

She sings of how the physical travels with us birthing the splendor of stars and galaxies, and how in this very moment we pass through the burning centers of stars, watching as they drift together to form galaxies.

She sings of how our conscious stream passes through exploding suns and of our joy and wonder as amidst all the gathering gases and dust, a new star is born and of our entrance into this star and of our presence as the physical gathers and coalesces. Her song tells us we are the watchers in the sun guiding the colliding masses, guiding the creation of our new home, our earth, a cocoon for the further march of evolution. She sings of the seas and the amoeba and the increasingly beautiful complexity, of the gradual drift of the physical until it takes a form, a body that opens as we join it. And all this happens in the now, in the present as we dance.

We watch the birth of this world, of this existence. She sings of our joining, our love and of our births and our deaths and of our many journeys back into the eternal Source, into infinite Being, the beyond of mind and matter, what we of mind and matter can only perceive as emptiness and yet is absolute potential, absolute creativity, absolute love. Her song tells me that existence is love.

She sings of our progress and our losses, of the wars and deaths, of the slow growth of our humanity and the many failures, and of this one among many, the final collapse that has brought us to this point.

The song fills me with sadness, and yet hope. She sings of our eternal being, of the love we carry in our minds and bodies, from the Source, from absolute Being, and how we are one always in the absolute, and of the opening of our true natures, our true selves.

And when she finishes we make love folded and floating in the shifting misty forms. Our total beings unite and flow together and in our union we become all the many worlds, the many dimensions. The mist flows smoothly over us blessing us in its warm caress, pressing us together. The world blesses us. The dream enfolds us in its own reality and becomes our reality.

We float out of the image as mist and as one. Gradually the mist parts and we stand as whole and separate selves.

Chapter Five

And then we sleep, folded in each other's arms. And dream again. But now our dreams wrap and tangle themselves mirroring the oneness of our bodies. We enter each other's dream and walk hand in hand into the golden light. We see the world as it truly is, underneath our waking reality. We see ourselves as we truly are in the final stages of our evolution. We see our fellow human beings in the glory of their true selves, love pouring from them and becoming part of and adding to the mist. We feel the mist as pure love and watch as it weaves the reality of our universe. We feel our love as a trace of the primal force of existence passing from the Source to us through all the layers of time.

There are the others. They reach into our dream, figures floating in the image. And we know that they are us. They are who we were and who we will be all in the now, our pure minds making our tortuous journey through the cosmos into our newly born universe. They are the many lives we have lived and they are us waiting for the final beings we will become, waiting for the perfection of this world and the final evolution so we together can flow into our perfected bodies. They tell us we are so close, so close. And finally we see the death throes of the old consciousness.

Lucia calls them the watchers and tells me, "In our ancient myths and religions we remember them as gods and angels who visit us. They seem other than us but they are us in our purely conscious state before we enter this universe and come to this earth in our present physical form. When some of you die you also become watchers and join in the effort to bring the Change. Those not ready to work for the Change go back into Being, to the Source to reconnect to their being consciousness.

Many of you possess a deeper memory, a membrance of the golden beings you are. Much deeper than ordinary memory, membrance seeps through the spacetime barriers of our universe to bring traces of the source into our lives. Love is one of those traces. It is the trace of the primal energy of existence, the drive of Being to create and extend existence. It is what pulls us out of the state of absolute potential into existence as a physical and mental entity. All acts of creation and beauty are traces of Being that membrance brings, half remembered remnants of the perfection of our true primal state along with the vibrations of that state.

Music is another trace of the vibrations that are part of our creation. Art, all of the colors and beauty that surround us are traces of this infinite urge. A trace of the primal creative urges that brings us into this world permeates all music, dancing, and images. Anything we do out of compassion carries the trace of the primal source.

Teachers have appeared who know something of the truth and have given birth to religions and philosophies. All religions and myths bear the traces of who we really are. But they have always been buried under the primitive fear that is part of this physical form, the fear of death."

She tells me this society is a mistake, a devastating mistake, led by the lost ones, the one who have lost all contact with their infinite selves, and find meaning only in their mistaken, desperate egos. They have turned this world into a cesspool, a world of hate and a world of lost dreams.

The Loss

We swim foamward
dream tendrils wrapped,
Everywhere Always
Floating
You lose, I lose you
As you sink
into existence
a density
a thickness
leaving me
almost and now
everywhere
you float
while I
thought born
wait.

The deep sings because you are there.

Chapter Six

When I awake I expect her to be gone, to have drifted back into the mists of the painting. But no, she lies beside me. I feel her body next to me, I feel her touch and I am lost in the feel of her. I am lost in the love of her and I lose myself to the love I feel.

And so we live our lives together. It is as though I have known her through all eternity. For many lifetimes I have come into this world without her. We first entered as a stream of consciousness pushed by the primal currents in a dance towards the new opening, the creation of our universe. In our journey through all the portals and entrances into this universe she traveled with me. We swam upwards together but at the point of entry she left me and sank down into the depths of Being. The emptiness of Being swallowed her again.

"Why could you not be with me? Why was I left to live all these existences alone?"

"I had to hold back. The world was not ready for us to be together and you needed to grow into this new consciousness by yourself. If I had come with you, you would not have sought your spiritual core. You would not have had the deep yearning that makes you a seeker. All of your lives have been dedicated to this seeking, this spiritual search."

She is here now as a fulfillment of the search, a search reaching completion. But the goal is infinite, because we are infinite in ways that are beyond what we can grasp in body or in mind. We are part of the untouchable mystery, the emptiness of the source that is truly infinite creative potential and gives birth to body and mind.

Finally she is with me, a loving, living presence, fully here. We live, as if in a cocoon, amidst all the darkness and repression, the so-called realities. In these early days together our love insulates us from the pain and fear of living in this dehumanizing regime. We move as if in a dream working and loving, learning the intricacies of our minds and bodies, experiencing the fullness of a deep eternal love, a love borne from eons of seeking and being together. She tells me, "Even though I have not been with you on this earth we have been together in our timeless existence. We have experienced all the lifetimes and consciousness of other worlds, all the glory of the burning suns. I have watched over you and been with your pure consciousness through all your many life times."

"How can this be?"

She answers, "In the old religions they believed that angels existed and that each person had a guardian angel. This is one of the traces that membrance brought to them. The angels of the old religions are actually the watchers; they are who we are before we enter this universe and take bodily form. Your guardian angel is really you and you sense that presence through time. Remember we are always in the now and the now encompasses all time, everything that has happened, is happening and will happen. While you are here physically in this lifetime you are also in the now, the state of pure consciousness. We are always connected in pure consciousness to the watchers and to each other. You are your own guardian angel. At this time the watchers are here to help us enter the next stage of evolution into this universe, into this world. They will come as we need them.

I have been with your pure consciousness through all your lifetime and watched over you. We have no ability to intervene directly in your life. We can only send inspiration and love. I know it is difficult to understand. But this is because it is difficult to understand the true nature of time, eternity and the Now. In this form we do not perceive time as layers of time with everything happening at once. But that is because in this universe we experience time as a series of happenings."

We know that this stage in our love cannot last forever. We know that soon we will have to face the reality of the world we live in.

Chapter Seven

I work in frenzy. The visions, the dreams, release torrents of images. They pour from me. I see forms, half hidden figures that seem ready to follow the mist into our world. But I also see portal like forms of light and color opening into that other world. I paint the beauty of these images in all their glory. I paint the beauty of Lucia in all her forms, forms that constantly shift and change. The puritanical regime has told me that what I paint is blasphemy, a contradiction to all we have been taught and all that is forced upon us. The Holy Enforcer tells us that we cannot love and make love, tells us of the ugliness and evil of our bodies, of the evil temptations of joy, of the evil of finding our own way.

We hear the loudspeakers blaring constantly from the compound. They constantly preach a gospel of forbidding and repression. We block out and ignore the voice that tells us we are evil and deserve punishment and that our natural selves are evil and should be repressed. When we walk through the streets, keeping ourselves hidden, we see men and women herded into the dark buildings with their dark covered windows, the men and women who are told they have sinned and must be punished. We hear the self professed virtues of the leader, the Holy Enforcer, who rules us in this world of hate and repression. No joy, no love, no sensuality or pleasure, no happiness. He preaches, "We are here only to seek salvation in another world, to escape this world of darkness and pain. This is our only destiny."

Ours is a destroyed world, a world of darkness and despair, the result of years of war and destruction. The irony is that it came when we were so close to building a new society.

I remember more and more of my past, even the knowledge I have accumulated over many past lives seeps into me. She tells me that in this new consciousness the boundary between life and death has softened. We no longer think of death as a final ending but as a transition into another form of being. It is as though the many layers of time are unfolding. I see only remnants, snatches of my history but they do tell me of the struggles that we as human beings have dealt with. They tell me of the many times we have had the material well being to move into a new way of existing. We come so close but always the old fears seize us. In particular they seize certain individual who grab power and turn our material successes into weapons and in their greed for power make war on the rest of humanity. It is almost a law that as we become close to a truly harmonious material existence there are those who seize power and destroy that existence. In their hate, hate of others, hate of the earth, hate of themselves, they continually pull us down to the level of a fight for survival. They feel no compassion, no love or care for anything or person outside themselves. The tragedy has not been just their madness but in the numbers of people who are willing to listen and follow them. And all this is ingrown fear, turning in on itself as the fear of loss of wealth, power and ultimately loss of life. By taking the material prosperity and the lives of others they think they can make themselves safe. But in the depths of their tormented minds they know they cannot escape, that death is always lurking, waiting for their time to end. And it is this terror of death that is the root of their hate.

This state that we live in is an outgrowth of all these fears. The regime took control after the wars. It was forced on us by the militias who began exterminating anyone who did not agree with them. They were the fundamentalists, the one who used belief in the literal truth of sacred texts, both religious and political, as a weapon of repression. Some of these writings were supposed to be records of the teachings of the great ones, of those who were close to Being, but their followers, because they were not ready, misinterpreted the teachings and took upon themselves the rewriting of the texts. They had not evolved to the point where they could use the teachings to bring about the great change. It is these rewritings and misinterpretations that the fundamentalists interpret literally and use as a justification for their actions. Even though there are traces of the great teachings still in these texts they are ignored and left out. They did not fit into the low level of consciousness of the fundamentalists.

They were the ones who claimed their right to horde as many weapons as they could. They claimed it was for self-protection but they began to use their weapons to exterminate anyone who did not agree with them, who did not have their notions of a sick morality. They also began to exterminate any politician who disagreed with them. Other politicians joined the insurrection. They used the so-called sacred texts to persuade many of the people, the fearful ones. They accumulated military leaders; they assassinated any leader who disagreed with the takeover. The slaughter became horrendous.

Certain corporations supported the takeover and provided more weapons. The coalition of religious fanatics and corporations gained military and political control. There was huge bloodshed and loss of lives. Many bodies were just buried in pits outside the city and covered over with bulldozers. The remaining people were herded into camps and forced to work. Eventually after the regime had complete control the people were assigned to compounds attached to the work places.

Chapter Eight

Where I come from is a mystery. I remember finding myself in a factory putting together materials for food and clothing. I passed the days in a stupor mechanically working. I don't remember how many years I lived this way. But often I felt the need for something more and I began to feel the impulse to create images, pictures that live inside me. This yearning burnt inside me as a desire I could only fulfill by leaving the compounds.

But in order to get food we need to work in the compounds. The food and other necessities are all in the control of the compounds. That is where the supplies are doled out, just enough to keep us alive and working. There is no other way to survive. It all comes from the compounds and from the regime.

As the regime became sure of its control it relaxed its watchfulness. Some of us began wandering the streets late into the night and searching in the deserted buildings. The buildings became a treasure trove of materials that helped us to survive and become more independent. With the collapse of the old government and the takeover by the coalition of religious fanatics most of what the previous civilization had produced was just forgotten and abandoned.

One night I found a supply of paints and brushes. Along with the art supplies I also found other tools and equipment and the search was on. We began searching through the buildings and numbers of us began gathering equipment that helped give us independence from the regime.

We began to pool together forming an independent brotherhood of sorts. We shared some of what we found with others who continued working in the compounds. They in turn shared their food and other necessities with us. A loose organization formed and many of us now live outside the compounds in the abandoned buildings. The repressive regime forces us to work together, to cooperate and to support each other.

We made the old buildings into what we call the warrens by knocking down walls and creating passages connecting one building to another. The regime feels so confident with its control of us that we are ignored. They believe they control all the food, clothes and other necessities, and they are so confident over their control of our minds that they do not suspect a small group of dissidents who are harboring a dream of freedom. We support and protect each other. Because of the supporters we have in the compounds, we are able to appear at work and fill out the proper work forms so that we are not detected. They falsify any reports to make it seem as though we are still part of the slave population. We have formed a reciprocal relationship with the compounds, giving them the technologies and equipment to produce more supplies. They in turn supply us with the materials we need to survive. In the direst circumstances the human spirit finds a way to bring us together. In this way the regime has helped to bring about the conditions for the further evolution of our consciousness.

There appear to be a number of such collectives growing throughout the city. This tells us that the regime is so smug and sure of its control that a growing number of collectives are able to scrape out a small amount of freedom.

In some of the buildings we have found not only old equipment but also old texts and writings. They show us how to repair and use some of the machines that belonged to the previous civilization. They also give us some inkling of the civilization that came before. We also found journals that describe the wars and the destruction that produced this regime.

The coalition of religious right and the corporations who used them to gain power and control had close ties to the military. With their own private armies and the military they were able to overpower any resistance. Many of the religious right horded weapons and guns and were able to go into the streets and kill any who tried to hide or who tried to put up any kind of guerilla resistance.

We spend nights reading these texts and journals to each other, freeing our minds from the rigid brain washing and mind control of the regime. The drive for freedom of mind and expression is so great in the human heart that we are willing to risk our lives for its pursuit.

Some of us: artists, writers, musicians, and scholars live and work in the old buildings. We have little spare time but our need to create gives us the energy to continue on in this work. We obey the regime in body but not in spirit. This is how we built "The Warren," where Lucia and I live. Where we are hidden and safe from the repression of the compounds.

From the outside the warrens appear as half-destroyed, abandoned buildings, but using supplies from the old civilization we have out fitted our lairs with the simple necessities that allow us to live and work.

But safety is not enough for us, especially for Lucia. "I came into this world to fulfill a purpose. The time is ripe for a change and we are the instruments of that change. Each of us must awaken to our heritage and role in the coming transformation.

As one of the watchers, your pure consciousness reaches through the layers of time, looking over you and trying to influence you. It is difficult because you are locked in the old mode of consciousness, the consciousness that came with your joining with the physical in this universe, with this earth. It is part of the evolutionary process that brings you into this form. It is based on the fear of death and the need for survival. It has forgotten where you come from and who you truly are, it has forgotten and lost the connection to true being, your divine self. It is as though you are asleep and must be awakened."

"But," I ask, "How do we fully awaken and how can we?" I feel that the process is beginning with me and some of the others, but what about the majority who live in the compounds? How hard and how long will it take for all of us to change?"

"It depends on how lost you have become in your survival mode. To some the combination of the fear of death and intelligence form a complex of emotions so deep they are not easily changed.

When consciousness joined with matter to become our physical form, it had to fit with our need to survive in this world. A consciousness based on fear and the need for survival and security turned in on itself and became greed for power and wealth, a kind of insanity that is now running its full course. This all consuming greed blocks any trace of your true selves

This regime is collapsing of its own paranoia. It has co-opted all belief in something beyond this world and turned it into the religion of a vengeful, punishing god. And yet in all of this, through the many twists and turns of our lives, of our evolution, we have always had traces of Being, the creative urge. Often it has been buried and at other times it starts to flower but each time the old consciousness takes hold. The fear of death, the paranoia, drives the traces under and a period of great destructions begins.

The great teachers have come and tried to bring you further in your evolution but they have only been partially successful. The fear of death and the fear for survival have often buried their truths. But the time has come and you are ready. Some of the watchers have waited eons for this development."

We struggle with the idea of how to bring the change about, how to bring an end to our desperate reality, how to share what we know, what we have been shown and what has brought her into this world. We will find a way.

We find others, others who feel the closeness of a new reality. We begin meeting and talking. Lucia sees my paintings as a tool, something we can use to motivate people. She believes there may be other possibilities; other ways of sharing our dream. Members of some of the other collectives meet in our warren. We begin to discuss the way to freedom, the way to begin to live the lives we are meant to live.

Chapter Nine

Josephus is a member of one of the other groups. He has never worked in the compounds nor has he ever lived there. He tells us that he was at one time a military leader high in the ranks of the regime. He was able to amass a large amount of wealth through his position.

We have known that the rulers do not obey or follow the teachings of the regime. Especially in the realm of sexuality. And he was no exception. The leaders had free reign over the men and women in the compounds, they were able to pick and choose whomever they wanted and either through coercion or by giving special favors they exploited the men, women and children in the compounds. Few of the victims had the power to refuse and many did not survive.

Josephus freely took part in these activities until he found a woman that he truly loved. They began to live together and were often seen as a couple. The fact that he did not quickly discard her created a scandal among the hierarchy. The scandal became even greater when they discovered she was pregnant. Natural pregnancies are strictly forbidden and even with the free reign given to members of the hierarchy Josephus could not escape the censure of his colleagues.

Josephus made enemies of the hierarchy because he did not display the merciless victimization that characterized the behavior of others. He too often showed compassion and consideration for those who were under his command. As a result he was respected and admired by his charges. This caused the other commanders out of jealousy and anger to become his enemies. They feared he would use his popularity as a means to gain more power.

They had just the weapon they needed when they discovered that the woman was pregnant and immediately plotted against him. Arguing in their usual hypocritical way that he was committing a sin they took her from him. One night as he and his love slept together they snuck into the bedroom and some held him down while others took her away. They planned to imprison and then execute him. He was to be made an example by the regime. She was sent to the childbearing compounds.

Members of his command were able to infiltrate the prison, overpower the guards and free him. They escaped from the compounds and began life in the deserted buildings.

Josephus was grief stricken and planned a way to find her and release her. He took a group of his followers and they seized control of the childbearing compound. Unfortunately the regime infiltrated the compound and attacked Josephus and his followers. Josephus managed to escape with a few followers and lived from that point onwards outside the compounds.

Over the years he gave up ever finding his love or the child she bore him. He had to reconcile himself to her death and the loss of his child. But his grief at her loss makes him a strong leader. He is skilled in finding ways to survive outside the regime. He lives for the day that the regime will end. He is a strong supporter and a leader of our movement and has organized us into a more effective force for our survival against the regime.

Chapter Ten

M ost of our efforts at this point are really aimed at mere survival outside the compounds. We remain hidden living on the outskirts of the city. But now we are ready to take action against the regime.

Lucia is strongly against any violent action. "Not only is the regime much stronger than we are militarily but any kind of armed insurrection will work against bringing about the Change. We have to find another way."

When Josephus sees my images he immediately realizes that they could be the instruments or at least an important component of what we can use against the regime. He tells us, "These images affect me so strongly; I know they will play an important role in the change. There is something in them that frees me from the blocks of fear and anger that have motivated me for so long and I recognize something much deeper is coming into our world. Not only do I realize the possibility of transformation but I feel the kind of change that the world needs."

The shapes and colors wrap around his mind pushing his thoughts and feelings in new directions. His meetings with Lucia cement these feelings. He senses her as a force, an elementary energy that will bring about the freedom of our people. He rallies the members of his group to support us. "These images must be shown to the world. They must be seen because of the effect they have."

Others in our group have been writing and composing music. We recognize the same power in their work. Our minds feed off of each other. "Why not have an art exhibit and performance," he proposes. So we plan. Can our work change the world? Can they remove the blinders that block our consciousness? Can we bring a new light into the world?

During this meeting Lucia speaks for the first time to the group. She stands before us in her full, powerful presence, a woman of this world and yet it is obvious that she comes from far beyond. She radiates a loving strength, inspiring us and filling us with the belief that we can succeed. She radiates all that we want to be and what we want the world to be. She is the embodiment of the Change our work brings into this world.

She tells us who she is and how she came to us. "I am new and yet old. I come out of now, beyond past, present and future. I am the past and the future. I always was and always will be, just as all the universes always were and always will be, just as you always were and always will be. We are creatures of all the universes, born out of love, because existence is love. And now I am in this body, in this physical self to be with you." A strange way of speaking, a strange way of being but she begins to open to us and to show us her full humanness.

Chapter Eleven

We make plans to have a public showing of our work. But if it is too public then the regime will be able to find and destroy us. We want to use the exhibit as a rallying point, a way to bring the city together.

Josephus has found another deserted building and managed to make it usable, but more importantly it has never been discovered by the authorities. "We are handicapped because we cannot make a public announcement of the show. We can only use word of mouth to spread the word. Tell only those we trust and have them tell only the people they trust and so on. The word will spread like a ripple through the city.

Tell our friends that there will be a major event at a future time. We will let them know when and where just before the event. They must be prepared to come at a moment's notice. We will use the warrens as the first line of communication. They will be an important link in our chain of communication, so when we announce the event, the information will spread down the chain from person to person. They must contact only those they trust. Even if a few supporters of the regime slip through, our work will so deeply affect them that they will fully embrace the movement. We must also be prepared to leave at any sign that the regime is attacking. I have chosen a building that has many passages that connect to other buildings so that it will be easy for us to evade any attempt to capture us."

Our life continues to flows smoothly and naturally in spite of the outward pressures of the regime. We eat, we walk, we make love, and yet it is beyond anything I have ever thought possible. It is hard to believe because we live in the same place, in the same world, but it has a newness, a new existence, a new way of being. It is something I have always yearned for, but could never find. And now it is here. It is here and it is beyond anything I have ever known, ever wanted and yet my day–to-day existence would appear the same to an outsider. So much of it has to do with Lucia and her presence, her inner sense of peace and joy. But I know that I am also changing from day to day.

Josephus sends out messengers to all of the warrens telling them where the show is and that it is tonight. They in turn contact their messengers, who then pass the word onto others. The word spreads.

Chapter Twelve

We bring our work to the gallery on the appointed day, and we begin making preparations. The gallery is in one of the cavernous basements of an ancient factory and has room for most of my paintings. On the night of the show someone guides each visitor down a series of steps and passages into the exhibition area.

I wait, wondering who will show up. Will it be our group or the regime? The basement connects through various passages to other basement so we do have escape routes. These are by-products of excavations made during the war.

Word of mouth successfully brings us an audience and visitors begin to trickle in. At first the audience looks silently and I wonder at the effect of the work. But slowly I see a change. They are transfixed. The transformation appears first in their faces. Then relaxation and joy come into their eyes. I am amazed at how quickly they feel the effect.

Throughout the evening our music plays giving an added dimension to the images. At intervals our poets stand beside the images and read. The words weave themselves into the music and the images. They tell of a lost land, a lost time and a yearning for a beauty that rests in our deepest hearts. But they also tell us of the coming of a new age where we humans will regain our rightful place in all the universes and beyond, a world where beauty and love reign supreme over the strangling fears of repression. Sensing the depth of what we are experiencing and the opening of a whole new view of our world and the universe we live in, we are filled with wonder and questions. We open to a sense of pure existence, pure being underlying our reality. We realize we are resonating on a new vibratory level and we ask Lucia about it.

"In Being, outside all the universes there is only vibration. There is no near or far, all is one. We are all one. The only differences are differences of vibration. Some of us are closer in vibration and we have a special affinity for each other.

Our world is part of a universe, which is one among an infinity of other universes, existing in the now of endless time. Each universe has a different set of vibrations. Light in our universe has a set of vibrations that are particular to this universe and create our particular space and time. This gives our universe the properties that allow stars to be born and die. Without these properties stars cannot exist and we cannot take this bodily form. Other universes have other sets of vibration giving them other properties. These are results of Being's natural urge to extend existence, the infinite urge that echoes down to us through membrance as love. What we experience as love is a membrance of the immense power of creation. All forces all matter, all emotions and thoughts are membrances of that power.

There is no end and no beginning. It is all one. As we develop, and I include myself now that I have come to you, we come closer to that infinite urge, that infinite beauty. We are creatures of the light, the light that comes to us from Being."

Our visitors go back into the warrens and compounds knowing something has taken hold of them, that they have been deeply changed and that they themselves can be instrumental in bringing that change out into the world. They want to share their inner transformation with the city. This is what we hoped for. This is the birth of a new belief in ourselves and in our future; that we will build a new society.

Chapter Thirteen

W e meet often at the gallery. It is a center, a sanctuary where people sing, dance and recite poetry, all bearing on the transformation.

But then I become aware that Lucia seems preoccupied. I see a distant look in her eyes, as though she is looking into her other world.

When I ask her she tells me, "I have been looking into the closest layers of time and I see the military marching on us. Because I have come directly out of the now I am not completely in this world. To you time is a series of events with one event happening after another. But outside this universe there is no time. Everything happens at once. However, you evolved in this universe and your evolution fits the laws of this universe. That is why in your present physical form this is confusing and seems impossible, but I experience time in layers with the layers of the past receding from me. I also see the future in layers moving further before me. The present is on the surface of all these layers. The past is fixed and unchanging. In this way I can know what the future holds. But it is constantly changing as we act in the present. What we do now constantly shifts the layers of the future. The immediate future closest to me does not have much chance to change and is more definite but as I see further ahead it constantly shifts so that all I can see are possibilities.

The regime is aware of us and ready to take action. They know of the gallery and are preparing to raid it in the near future. This is becoming increasingly more probable. Send out warnings to all of the warrens and particularly to Josephus."

The word goes out and we begin moving all the equipment and images through the passages. We work long into the night. We trust that Lucia will be able to see when the attack is imminent. At the last moment we cover up all the passages so that the regime does not know how we are able to escape. Josephus and his followers are working up to the last moment to cover our tracks. Lucia senses the approaching troops and warns Josephus to leave immediately. To our relief Josephus and his group escape at the very last moment but the regime is now aware and is searching for them.

Lucia and I take refuge in our warren and the others move to their particular warrens. The regime has disrupted our movement and we are now fragmented. We send messages back and forth to each other, but I miss the sense of community we had when we could meet at the gallery. I feel we are at a standstill.

We feel fairly safe for the time being. Josephus is the only one that the regime is aware of and is searching for. I have always led a hidden life away from the eyes of our repressors and they have no idea where the images come from. I hadn't publicized my work nor associated myself with it. We feel secure in our anonymity. To be unnoticed can be a blessing.

I continue with the work finding them magically finished in the morning. Did I create the images or did she? What is her role? They seem to just appear. I know that they come from some deep level inside me, but it is a level beneath my waking awareness. The choices I make in my work come from that level and my work just seems to happen.

In many ways the paintings mirror our relationship. I feel her love so strongly and yet I see how she responds with deep affection for everyone around her. The intensity of our love grows with each moment we spend together. We feel increasingly stronger and more caring in our love for life, our friends, and the whole of our existence. It is a universal love that grows stronger as our personal love grows. She radiates universal love, and her presence creates the atmosphere of love that surrounds us.

I ask Lucia how it could be. She holds me close and kisses me. Her kiss fills me with the deepest love for all of existence and yet at the same time I also feel the powerful emotional and sexual pull of our desire. It is as though the love of all humanity expresses itself through our bodies. We respond to each other with ever increasing intensity. I feel a deep love for others and yet my response to her radiates through me taking possession of every part of my body. I want to sink into her and become so close that we meld into one ecstatic being. I feel the same from her. She looks into my eyes and tells me how deeply and strongly she loves me.

After we make love we lay in close embrace, arms and legs wrapped wound tightly, enjoying the closeness of our bodies and the pure sense of being together.

I ask her why these moments are so special. "How does our love fit this deep sense of being that is so universal?"

"Our world outside of time is made of universal love, the kind we feel here but outside in our other existence, in the now, it stretches back through eternity to the source. It echoes the energy that must constantly created. The love we feel is a true reflection of that creative force.

We are universal beings connected to each other through the source, to Being. It is one aspect of who we are but there is also a unique personal aspect to all of us. In this particular existence, in this physical form we also feel deep personal love. It is as though all existence is an infinitely faceted jewel. Each of us is a facet reflecting the world from our particular viewpoint, our particular perspective. We are both the jewel and the facet. We contain both the universal and the personal aspect. Our love for each other is a reflection of that unique personal aspect. It is what gives the world the richness and diversity that nourishes. Both the unique and the universal enrich one other. When we make love I feel the wholeness of the all coming through us. It is a rare and precious gift our bodies give us.

Think of one of your paintings or any masterpiece. The details, the smaller elements enrich the whole painting, and the whole gives the details, the unique elements a place to live. They enrich each other and without either the painting would not have the effect or bring the response it does.

Because you and I have almost the same set of vibrations, we have this affinity for each other and that is why you paint as you do, and why your images pull me into this existence."

Chapter Fourteen

These are the safe moments wrapped in the soft refuge of our love, but tensions from the outer world increasingly intrude into our lives. We must hide our love and its expression or we will be arrested and punished. Lucia because she is a woman is especially in danger. Except for the street girls, the regime restricts almost all women to the compounds. To go out into the streets she must pose as a street girl, and we men must pose as sex seekers. This is the only way we can be seen outside the warren. Usually however, we move through the city using the passages between buildings. As much as possible we avoid open space.

The regime continues to increase as an ever present threat and causes us to be constantly wary. It threatens every aspect of our existence. We want the freedom to express our love and our love of others to the whole world. We want the freedom to create beauty and celebrate the joys of life. We want to create a life and a world that keeps the promise of a joyful and loving existence, of care for each other and the freedom to fulfill our destiny as the human aspects of Being. We are part of the creative force that brought our world into existence and we want to be part of that continuing creation. We are here to perfect the physical world, to perfect our minds and bodies. That is our true human destiny.

But the regime is always with us. How do we free ourselves from its crushing suppression of any sign of loving expression? How do we free ourselves from a regime that claims absolute power over our minds and bodies?

Chapter Fifteen

When I see the preoccupied look on Lucia's face I know that something is coming. I know she sees something is going to happen. She warns me that the regime is about to strike again and that it will be soon. We immediately send warnings to the other warrens hoping that they reach them in time. We pack our belongings and with the help of others move the images.

Finally in the night she tells me that they are here and about to enter our building. We hear the door come crashing down. We grab our bags and enter the passages with barely enough time to cover-up our escape. I am sure they will be found but it may give us more time to make our escape.

We travel through other studios and living spaces picking up others as we move from unit to unit. Finally we enter an alley and find our way through a series of buildings into an adjoining street. From there we enter another block of buildings making our way to what must have been the industrial center of the city. We avoid the streets and alleys because we can hear helicopters flying above. As we hear them approach we scurry into nearby buildings until we hear them move on. We travel in this way for hours. The factories are on the outer edge of the city.

As dawn approaches and just when we reach the point of exhaustion we notice an open door in one of the buildings. A young man signals us inside. We enter and he leads us deeper into the building and finally down a series of steps into a cavernous room. We come to rest surrounded by a group who quietly watch as we find a place to rest. Looking around the room I notice many of our images hanging on the walls. Josephus emerges from the crowd.

"Because of your warning we knew that an attack was imminent and we were able to rescue most of your work. The regime attacked many of our warrens at the same time, but most of us escaped and found our way here."

"We need to preserve this work. It is a fundamental part of the movement. Your work and the work of other writers and musicians are the only ways we have now of reaching the people. It tells us that there is another meaning to life, but more importantly it shows us who we are and where we come from. It tells us that we are infinite beings and part of the source, the center of all creativity, the source of existence. And within that place in ourselves we can find the peace, harmony, and love that are part of our heritage and belong in this world. It is up to us to bring this harmony into the world and to make the world a mirror of what we find in ourselves.

We know we have to resist this tyranny and we are ready, but how can we? How do we use this work to continue to free ourselves and others? I believe that if others could see our work they would follow us. We have the means to print copies of the images and writings and spread them throughout the city."

Lucia nods, "It is a good beginning but we need to do more. We need to perform and dance and spread our work in all directions from wherever we can. We need to find a new way of freeing our minds and bodies. We need to go deeper into the infinite love that is who we are. We need to go deeper into the traces of existence that brought us into this world. That is where we come from and that is what we carry within us. We have to let it come through us, not only in the images, not only in our writings, not only in our music and dance, but in the way we live, in the way we love and care for each other." And she moves throughout the room touching and looking into the eyes of all those she comes in contact with. They in turn touch and look into the eyes of those close to them. It is as if an electric current passes through the room. Men and women join in a weaving, winding movement. They begin a chorus, chanting and using their voices as instruments and drums.

Because of our escape and our ability to come together we find new hope and confidence. We have won a small victory over the regime. With all their weaponry and power they have not been able to eradicate us. We dance until we are free of all the fears and repression we have suffered throughout our lifetimes. Finally we are exhausted and fall into a deep sleep.

When we wake we remember and tell each other about our dream, a collective dream, a dream of strange beautiful beings, who speak to us and welcome us into a new world. They tell us they are with us always and will help us find the life we want. The dream is the same for all of us and yet each person sees it from a different perspective and each person's telling of the dream brings out a more complete and richer vision for us to live with.

This is the true spirit of the resistance. With this vision we feel a new commitment to change the world. It reenacts our move out of the source and our journey through the universe. It tells us we are a work of creation carrying all the traces of Being. It tells us that we carry a core deep within ourselves. We realize that our music is a trace of the primal force that pushed us out of the emptiness of pure being into consciousness. It tells us that all of the forces we experience are variations of that first primal force. All of our love is a trace of the primal principle of existence, the urge to become. All love: romantic, erotic, motherly, fatherly is a trace of the primal urge to extend existence.

And this is what we must use to free ourselves from the darkness of our world. Somehow we have to continue to enlighten ourselves and others to who we are and where it is we come from. The world waits through the night and tomorrow is a new dawn, a new beginning.

Chapter Sixteen

The next day some of us return to the compounds and to the work assigned to them by the regime. Others begin the work of printing the images and writings. Lucia moves constantly through us as we work. Her presence is a source of energy and light constantly inspiring us.

I continue producing new images, and the writers and musicians continue with their work until we are ready. We begin bringing it out into the open. When I look at the collection of my paintings I see that they are almost one painting. They do differ but each complements the others. Each adds a distinctive element to the whole. And this is true with our poetry and our music. It is one continuous work with the thread of our vision running through it. Even though the police search ever more frantically for us, we find ways to make the work public without discovery, to bring our work out into the world.

We move one or two at a time into the streets and then back into the compounds with help from our supporters. Each of us carries small packets of printings and without being noticed passes them to people we meet. Some take the packets and pass them to others. We create ripples of activity and throughout the succeeding days the ripples spread. But it is slow.

Occasionally we find buildings, ancient and deserted where we celebrate and dance, where we recite our poetry. Those who are not still in the compounds now occupy the old factory buildings and live deep in the basements. We move all of our equipment to these hidden refuges. We use passages that we keep hidden and this prevents us from being captured.

Lucia warns of any imminent raid and as the time for a raid approaches she tells us where it will occur. We have enough time to be sure our passages are covered and move deep into the basements. For many hours we sat in silence not daring to move and barely able to breathe as we hear the approaching sirens and the boots of the police and military overhead. Lucia tells us when it is safe and we go back to our work.

But it all seems too slow and too little. In spite of our ability to survive and our effort to spread the work, we seem to be barely making a dent in the control the regime wields. Our progress is much too slow. How can we move more quickly against the machines and weapons of the regime?

The Holy Enforcer begins using loudspeakers to excoriate us. "They are filthy vermin who open their bodies to lust and degeneracy. They threaten the purity of the temple."

The diatribes go on. We don't know how effective they are. We worry that the biases of the large masses of people are so deep that it is hard for us to reach them. When people are indoctrinated at birth they accept it as the absolute truth.

The Holy Enforcer repeats his notion of the filth of the body, the bestiality of sexual love and the need for control and repression to contain our animal nature.

He is often seen with his collection of young boys. He tells us that they are being groomed under his tutelage as future leaders. Women are purposely excluded from leadership as creatures of temptation and sin. Lucia remarks at how repression bends our natural desires into the need to exploit the young and weak. "The love between any two people is a sacred thing, but this is not love. It is the exercise of brute power and control."

Chapter Seventeen

L ucia continues her evolution as a physical being during this time and truly begins to perfect her bodily form. I don't realize how ephemeral her presence has been until I see the changes. Her body is evolving to become more compatible with her consciousness. Her grace and beauty become increasingly more evident and more affective. Her sensuality makes it a joy to be in her presence. She inhabits our space with the full command of a goddess and yet has an earthy sexual presence that excites and intrigues. I grow to want to be with her just to feel her presence and as that happens we grow even closer physically. I never imagined that we could be any closer but we now move in a realm far beyond what has existed in our usual human sphere.

Her enjoyment of our lovemaking has become so unrestrained, passionate and intense that I feel we inhabit the same body. It is the physical embodiment of the oneness of the other world. We move to a vibratory level that goes to the very core of our being. In our deepest passion we travel into another existence- the place she comes from. This seems strange to me, but as it happens more and more I begin to accept it. I feel lifted out of myself and transported with her into the other dimension. She talks often of how this is happening and the joy it brings her.

"My physical self is growing and I am becoming more and more compatible with the physical aspect of myself. This is a joy we don't experience when we are in pure consciousness, it needs our bodies. They have their own knowledge and experience to give us. After all they are made of elements that have existed and transformed since the very beginning of your universe. They came out of Being as the physical stream along with the conscious stream. The union with our consciousness makes all of this part of our total perception. It is a special gift from Being and traces back to the primal impulse that creates the physical."

Chapter Eighteen

I know she also communicates with the others, the ones she calls the watchers. She says, "the watchers are humans in purely conscious form before we join with the physical, before the physical develops enough to be compatible with these particular forms of consciousness. We come out of our conscious form, part of a stream of consciousness. But a physical stream also forms and travels with us. The watchers are us before the joining, some remain back as pure consciousness until the time is right, until they feel that the physical realm is ready for their joining, until there is a physical form with their similar vibratory level"

The images that come in the night trigger Lucia's entry. She is both the recipient and the creator. Because our vibrations are so close we are meant for each other and she uses the images as a gateway between worlds. And because we are so close she enters my mind through my dreams and helps me form the images. In this way she continually recreates her physical form. But the longer she is with us the less dependent she becomes on the images.

This is not the first time she has been in this world. Her other entries come in the usual way, through an ordinary birth, the way the rest of us enter this world.

"As a physical being develops in the womb it becomes increasingly compatible with the our form of consciousness and when body and mind are completely ready it releases itself out of the womb and with the first breath the process is complete. It becomes a conscious human being. As the baby grows the fit between body and mind grows stronger. This continues throughout our lives but until we are transformed it is not complete, our evolution has to continue. When we have gone as far as we can in our present state towards transformation, our consciousness leaves our body. We either travel back into Being or remain as a watcher waiting for the next stage in our evolution. At a high level of evolution we move freely from the physical to pure consciousness at will according to the need to continue our evolution."

"I am many people and live in many times but in pure consciousness I experience them all simultaneously. Everything that happens, every event in the cosmic tree occurs simultaneously. Just as to a beam of light everything happens at once. Light is the key, it contains all of the now and all is now."

I am slowly beginning to understand what she tells me. It resonates with a deep inner knowledge. Even though my ordinary language holds me back, I realize that the images and memories from my past lives and experiences are flowing into my conscious awareness. I now have a deep reservoir of experiential knowledge, I can tap into.

"Your language developed to describe events at the particular vibrations of this universe. It describes a sequential time and a separation of space. Outside in the cosmic tree there is no time, there is no separate place, it is all one, and it is all now. This is hard to comprehend because your body has formed in this universe and as this universe developed with its particular vibrations, separate time and separate space became its nature. Light no longer moves instantaneously. It has slowed to its present speed. This is part of the development of your space and time.

Before the ban scientists found evidence of the unity of space and time. But with the bans this knowledge is forbidden. The teaching of the evolution of nature is also forbidden. The regime has either lost this knowledge or keeps it hidden.

As physical evolution occurs it becomes more compatible with consciousness. With the joining, consciousness also evolves and develops with the experience of its new physicality. Realize that every particle in your body at this very moment is travelling through many universes and many stars and has its impressions and experiences and these now are part of your consciousness. We are in the process of a new transformation of mind and body.

All the repression we now experience with this regime is the last throes of an old consciousness- an old way of being. In its final efforts to preserve itself it has become more fanatical and more repressive."

Again I resonate to what she tells me and am slowly leaving old ways of thinking behind. I know that at this time I am becoming more fully aware of my deep nature. I am changing. The images, the presence of Lucia become a constant transformative force. Her singing, her way of being, her love permeates our atmosphere. We record her songs and send them out into the world.

Chapter Nineteen

W e have access to loud speakers and set them up throughout the city. We play a game of cat and mouse with the regime, constantly moving them before the regime comes to tear them down. They are part of a cache of old equipment that was abandoned in the basement of some of the deserted buildings, some of which were factories and businesses that were left and abandoned after the fall, after the wars. Our presses and most of our other equipment come from such supplies. Much of the equipment is much more advanced then what the regime has and it has lost the information to make and repair them. The technology and ability to make such machines was destroyed in the slaughter that came with the destruction.

We find old manuscripts and books that teach us to repair and use the technology. Some members of Josephus's group have become competent technicians who maintain and develop our technology. In many ways we have become technologically superior to the regime. They were interested in only the weapons and machinery that would help them maintain control of us. However, they do have helicopters and motorized vehicles which they are barely able to maintain.

We are able to run the presses and other equipment for a few days before the regime finds them and tears them down. Lucia always warns us that a raid is coming and we move on and find other sites. Some of us are caught and disappear but we continue. For any that we lose there are others to replace them. There is something in the human heart that wants to hear our message, that knows there is something beyond the hate and fear that the regime constantly forces on them.

Chapter Twenty

The struggle continues. We put our message of love and hope against the raw force and power of the regime, our love and care for each other against the entrenched power interests that use us as fodder for their machines.

The message is spreading much faster than I thought possible, and when I ask Lucia how and why, she tells me that the watchers are also influencing us. They are working throughout city. This is another indication that the time is right. The watchers are beginning to feel the pull of our evolution. They are beginning to feel the rightness of entering our dimension and becoming fully human. And in spite of the repression and the banning we are growing.

"It is the natural order to bring these energies and love into this universe. To perfect and extend being is the extension of the natural force of existence. It is only thorough this change that our world will ever know peace. This has to occur at an individual level. We have to feel the power of this love and use it as our only means of transformation. This is the only way the change will occur. We have to love even the repressors, and with that love we can bring about the change. In any other way the old ways of thinking will return."

"How can you be sure?"

"I'm not absolutely sure but just as the past is always present in the now, so is the future. But as I have told you it appears as a changing vision of possibilities. The now is what we can immediately experience. What we do now is making the future we want an almost certainty. If we hold onto our love and care we will act in a way to complete our vision."

I begin to understand, and the sweetness of her being makes what is mysterious seem so real and so loving. I am constantly drawn to the mystery of this other reality she brings to us. I feel her love as a constant force, an energy that recreates our being, and constantly changes how I am, and how I perceive the world. This is true for the people around me. Our circle of friends grows. I notice the change, the love that emanates through their eyes and the care they have for each other. I feel that same love growing inside me.

Chapter Twenty One

At times Lucia seems to evaporate and fade into the images, into the shapes as I paint. The images are vibrations of different frequencies in the form of colors and shapes. Because of Lucia's influence the images contain just the right vibrations that allow her to pass through an opening into the timeless realm. I don't understand why at this particular time images have this ability and why they pass through me. She replies that when the time is right certain individuals tap into the coming transformation. Our consciousness is lifting to a new level of vibration.

"Outside all of the universes, we enter the cosmic tree. There is no space and time; there is only vibration, an infinite variety of vibrations and these, through Being, create the various universes. This universe has a particular range of vibrations and these set the time, space and other characteristics that give this universe its properties. If this universe had different properties stars could not exist and you could not exist in your particular human form.

In Being, you and I are very similar. This is why I am drawn to you and why your paintings create the openings that allow me to travel back and forth between our worlds. We are very close in vibration. But your vibrations shift and are affected by your existence in this universe and by your experiences during this lifetime. Up to this time they have not allowed me to enter. The vibratory levels are now changing for you and the other people in our movement. This is bringing on the transformation."

Mostly the images aren't anything that resembles our world. They are effervescent and dreamlike. They have a certain rhythm to them. They are nothing I paint consciously but come from a deeper level.

I ask her about this. "Why are they so powerful and moving? When I look at them they are just shapes and forms, but they carry a strong emotional impact- they have a meaning that goes far beyond any other images I have made. But it is a meaning I cannot frame in words. When I think I am beginning to understand them, their meaning slips away"

"They are protoforms." She answers. "The world comes at us as vibrations, as waves, and according to our vibratory level we put them into images. The images work with our language and our language is part of what we perceive. We are co - creators in this reality. As our vibrations change so will our reality and so will how we perceive and change our reality."

I feel the changes occurring and know what I need to do. I need to become even closer to the other world. I need to portray traces of our being that stretch back to our creation, and bring the many lifetimes we travel from the source into this universe. I need to make my work full of who we are and where we are going and I need to spread my work throughout the city.

When I tell Lucia. She answers, "The time has not yet come. Your world is not ready for the full impact of the traces. You need to let the development go further."

Chapter Twenty Two

A t this time we are moving from deserted building to deserted building barely evading the police. Lucia's ability to read the future keeps us from being captured.

"Let me use your images to explain how I experience time. Look at them. The top layer, closer to the present is clear. As you move into the deeper layers they become less clear, this is how the future appears to me, except our present actions affect the future causing the layers to shift. The future appears as constantly shifting layers of possibilities. The further I see into the future the more the layers change. The closer we are to the present the more stable the layers are."

We are able to evade the police and we are able to warn our friends and compatriots of any attack. Also increasing numbers of military and police are deserting the regime and joining us.

Lucia is very good at seeing into them and seeing who are truly part of the transformation and who are spies. We evade the spies by giving them false addresses, false meeting places. We lead them on, giving them misinformation.

The regime becomes increasingly threatened as we become more successful- as our numbers grow. As they feel the threat their violence grows and their repressive measures become increasingly harsher.

They try torture. But those who are captured have learned the ability to leave their bodies and return to Being. Many of us have evolved to this stage of the transformation. When we have completely evolved, we no longer need to die but at a point where we are finished with the meaning of our particular lifetime we just drift away and leave our bodies behind. The line between life and death becomes softer.

But I am still saddened by our losses; we have lost many who are close to us. Lucia tells me that even though they are not in physical form they are still close to us. "They have joined the watchers and will be with us when we need them."

Chapter Twenty Three

We hear the voice of the Holy Enforcer, a constant presence in the compounds and in streets. "These animals become increasingly dangerous. We need to stop them. Our divine powers will cast them into the pits. We are the ordained ones, the ones who have been chosen to rule over these beasts and we will destroy them. Our God is a vengeful and punishing God and we are the instrument of his divine will."

He projects his anger and fear into the street but we have become immune. Unfortunately those around him have no protection from his insane rage.

His screaming echoes through the palace. The young boys who share his bed freeze. They know his anger will turn on them and they remain silent, hoping for a change in his mood. They are often the recipients of his so- called divine wrath. But he becomes increasingly agitated. Something is changing in the world and he doesn't understand it. He feels control is slipping away from him. He believes in using the notion of sin and punishment to control, but these weapons no longer work.

Even rationing food is not working. The people are no longer willing to work for a bare sustenance. Production is slipping. The food and other necessities rationed out at the work places are barely enough to keep the people alive. This is not out of necessity. There is plenty to go around. The regime uses its control over food to keep us dependent. We break this dependence by raiding the warehouses and creating our own supply. Much of the production of the workers now finds its way into the basement of our buildings.

People are beginning to gather in the streets. But as soon as the police come close the crowds quickly disperse. Even the police and military become infected with the desire for freedom. They no longer pursue us with their previous zeal. We know they are releasing the ones they do capture.

The Holy Enforcer brings his commanders before him. "Why have our arrests and executions dropped off," he asks them.

"The soldiers don't have the will to kill and maim to enforce our bans." They tell him.

His rage becomes uncontrollable, "We need to force them. We need a quota of killings; anyone who does not meet this quota will be shot or imprisoned. And if you do not enforce my regulations you will be shot. I will no longer tolerate this insubordination. Now get out."

After they leave he goes into the bedroom and calls for his favorite boy. He is nowhere to be found. He has left the palace. All searches for him fail. The Holy Enforcer falls on the other boys beating and kicking them. They try to flee but the doors are locked. Some try to fight back but he clubs them into unconsciousness. He falls collapsing onto the floor.

Chapter Twenty Four

The struggle continues. We know from the increasingly desperate violence that the regime is in trouble. It is at this time that the watchers begin speaking to us. Their inspiration and presence give us new hope. Many of our friends are disappearing and we feel their loss. But even in our sadness we know they are safe and present in Being and in time will reenter our world.

But where do we go from here? We need something else, a new way of getting our message to the people. A new instrument, a new vision, something they can see.

And we suffer another serious loss. Josephus is captured and taken to the palace. Josephus, besides being a friend and often a protector, has been one of the most dedicated leaders in our organization. He is one of the most evolved of our group and we are sure that he can prevent himself from being harmed. But we miss him.

The watchers give us a new direction. With their help we can manipulate light on a large scale and send images into the atmosphere. We are able cover the skies with an image that will work on the consciousness of anyone who see it. In this way we will reach the large numbers of people needed to transform our city into a city of light. With this new hope in our hearts we begin planning.

We assemble the equipment needed. We have to move into the streets more frequently and things became increasingly more dangerous. Lucia seems oblivious to the danger. She takes much greater risks by going into the streets more often.

To create the vision, we need to assemble large numbers of people and watchers and this takes a huge amount of organization. I worry incessantly about her and what could happen. She seems to want to be captured.

Chapter Twenty Five

And then it does happen. Rumors have circulated about a presence- a leader who galvanizes the movement. As she leaves one of our buildings The police surround her. They must have recognized her importance because they immediately take her into the presence of the The Holy Enforcer. As they lead her into his throne room, members of the government gather to see the confrontation. She appears completely unafraid.

The Holy Enforcer demands that she stand before him and as she walks before him, he scowls. He is not used to having someone who is so completely uncowed in his presence.

"Who are you and where do you come from," he asks. She remains silent, looking at him. "I demand an answer," he screams.

"Your time has ended," she replies, "you cannot stop the transformation. It is here and it has begun."

His face contorts and turns purple with rage. He is a bully and when someone confronts him, he feels only fear. His fear turns easily to rage and he stands and descends down to her. He strikes at her swinging his fist attempting to crush her. She easily evades his attack. He charges again at her. Again she moves so swiftly, he misses and falls. "Grab her," he commands and a number of his cohort leap at her.

She evades them moving swiftly with dancelike grace, slipping between them until finally she stops and lets them stand her before him. She begins laughing. His crown askew and his robes in disarray, he looks a pitiful creature. She laughs again. "You cannot stop what is about to happen. Your power, your violence is futile against what is happening."

He strikes at her face but his fist passes through her. Her face turns into mist and then reforms. He strikes again and again and everywhere he hits her she disappears and then reappears. He goes into a fury and reigns blow after blow on her. She merely evaporates wherever he strikes and reforms. Finally in frustration, He screams, "Hold her still," then turns on her captors and begins to savagely strike them. They defend themselves and move away from her. She begins to walk through the room. Others try to grab her but their hands just pass through her and when she reaches the large barred doors she merely walks through them into the daylight.

Chapter Twenty Six

We group together trying to come up with a plan to free her. We are willing to undertake any of what we know is a futile attempt, a suicide attempt to free her.

It is at this time that the watchers begin entering our world. Many of our friends reappear and with joy I see that Josephus is among them. They tell us to be patient. And so we wait.

Josephus speaks to me about our past. He has resolved the mystery of his lost wife and the child she bore him. By traveling into a past layer he was able to comfort her as she lay dying. He also resolved the issue of who I am and my past life. "You are the son she bore me. They took you away and raised you in the compounds. We have been bound together through your lifetime.

Do not worry about Lucia. She is far more powerful than any of our repressors. She will be with us soon." It is now clear why Josephus and I have had a special connection.

She floats through the door as a golden mist and takes on her physical form as though nothing has happened. As she stands before us the mist evaporates. She is the culmination of all we as humans can become. But to me she is my being, my life. All my fear at having lost her turns into tremendous relief and joy. We rush into each other's arms and I feel the rush of love that is the essence of who we are.

She appears more radiant than ever and I am struck again by her grace and poise. I feel the effect she has on the others. Her presence fills the room with creative power- a love that brings out the full strength within us. We know who we are and where we come from. We know our role in the transformation and grow to fulfill that role. We know that we will succeed and we will succeed with love and care.

I ask her, "If you have this affect on us why it is that The Holy Enforcer does not feel it."

"Because of fear. He knows on a really deep level that his time is ended and his fear fills him and blocks any influence of love. There are others who are so enmeshed in their power and who fear that loss so deeply that they cannot be reached. We can only hope that we can reach the people they control. Some fear him so much that they are blocked, but there are others who we will reach. I felt it when they tried to grab me. It will take time. The blocked ones will eventually become isolated and fade away. We can only hope that we reach most of them before they damage us and our movement. The future is unclear. Most of it depends on our ability to free ourselves from our own fear." We immediately continue our planning.

Chapter Twenty Seven

I n the citadel The Holy Enforcer does indeed feel the fear underlying his rage. He cannot understand what has happened.

"It has to be the work of Satan. She is a demon. Alert the people and tell them that we have a demon among us and she has power over the rebels because of their wickedness. Our world is in the possession of demons and they must be stopped. Any gatherings must be fired upon. We will enforce a full time curfew so that only those with special permission will be on the streets. Anyone else will be shot. I know we have no more room in the prisons.

Shoot them and dump the bodies in the pits outside the city."

And so the regime becomes even more violent. This increases the danger at a very critical time because we need to move out onto the streets to bring on the vision and we need a large gathering, almost everyone in the group. We think about moving to the hills outside the city and projecting from there. But there is still the problem of moving large numbers through the city without being detected. If we can remain undetected until a short time before the projection then we can increase our chances of success. We will have to move almost individually, maybe in twos and threes. The more people we have the stronger and more vivid the image will be. But first we need a site. And we know time is critical. The longer we wait the more dangerous it becomes for all of us. If we take too much time the regime will crush us.

We send a few scouts into the hills to find a site and we wait for their return. Meanwhile we continue with our old means of communication: images, writings, and performances in the old deserted buildings. We gather more followers but we are losing more people. Do we have enough time to project the image?

And then another tragedy strikes. Our scouts have not returned. Do we send more out, or wait hoping they will return. We wait.

Chapter Twenty Eight

Some of our group- the former soldiers want to fight back. And the arguments begin. Lucia tells us that only through peace and persuasion can we win, "They have to feel our love. Even if we could win pitched battles we would end up with just another form of repression. We have to produce a shift in consciousness. That is the only way the transformation can occur."

The arguments continue and some cannot be convinced. Especially as we lose more and more of our loved ones and the regime becomes increasingly hateful and violent. We try to persuade them, but again fear is our enemy.

They become blocked. And the images and work cannot affect them.

One of the group claims he knows of an entrance into the palace that is not as strongly guarded. He is also one of the main arguers for an attack. "We cannot let this regime get away with killing and capturing us. We are cowards if we do not strike back."

Our numbers have grown so great that Lucia and the other watchers cannot see into all of our members. We are becoming victims of our own success. Lucia has not had a chance to know this new member. He has remained obscure up until this moment. She does however see that a disaster is coming. We continue arguing but a group splinters off from us and we lose contact with them. We have no way of preventing what we are sure will be a disaster.

Finally the group gathers their weapons and goes out into the streets. Their idea is to move against the citadel in a sneak attack. Lucia again sends out a warning and tries to stop them, telling them that the future predicts disaster. But again they cannot be dissuaded and in the darkness of night they move into the streets.

They plan to create a distraction that pulls the regime's main force away from the citadel.

The results are a tragic set back. We lose hundreds of followers. The regime is not distracted and sends a small force to capture our followers. They then lay in waiting for the attack on the citadel. It is a massacre; even the leader is killed in the slaughter. We realize that he was sent by the regime to create this disaster.

But as bad as this loss is there is another consequence. We see a decline in new recruits. The violence has disrupted our transformational process. For the first time I see sadness in Lucia's face. She feels the losses deeply, but even more she regrets the disruption in our evolution, and the breakdown of the process that changes consciousness.

"I am concerned that we are not ready for the changes that could come. Perhaps we were wrong, perhaps this is the wrong time."

"But if not now when," I reply. She moves silently out of the room and I am suddenly concerned with losing her. Without her we will lose everything we strive for.

We stop speaking to each other, I feel her begin to slowly dissolve. Each day she became less and less substantial. Each day she becomes more and more transparent. I try to hold her, to make love to her but even her touch has a quality of nothingness, of emptiness.

Chapter Twenty Nine

Either emptiness or something else contained in the emptiness. Something beyond consciousness or physicality which in my ordinary mode of consciousness I cannot touch. She is moving back into the emptiness of Being. Is it a retreat, a going back to the source for more strength and more resolution or are we going to completely lose her? In my sadness I try to reach out to her but to no avail. She is here but gone. The days rush by. We are immobilized. It seems like the end. I find refuge in my painting hoping that in the images something that can save us will emerge.

And then after a few days suddenly she is back. She seems to have a new strength and at about that time one of the scout's returns. We have lost the others but she did find a site. On a hill close to the city there is an amphitheatre opening out to the city. It can hold a large number of people and we will be able to project the vision into the skies above the city. We can move in small numbers into the forests behind the amphitheatre and hide. At a given moment we will move into the space and begin projecting. We know that helicopters patrol the hills so the projection would have to begin quickly.

And so we begin. Each night a small contingent moves into the streets and travels house by house towards the hills. We calculate that it will take at least seven nights for several hundred people to reach the forests. After seven nights Lucia, the watchers and I begin moving through the houses and streets.

The most likely place for an ambush is at the city's borders in the open fields before we enter the forest. As we move into the open, a bevy of helicopters moves towards us. Have we been discovered? We drop to the ground hoping the short scrub will hide us. They pass over us and I breathe a sigh of relief. But then they turn around and circle back towards us. One drops close to the ground. They have seen something and are coming to check. We are in mortal danger. If Lucia and the watchers cannot get to the amphitheatre then we cannot project the vision. The watchers turn on their back and begin staring at the sky immediately above us. As the helicopter comes closer a haze rises from the ground and the haze becomes a slightly thicker and higher brush covering us. The helicopter flies over and joins the others and they continue onward. We are safe.

We continue crawling through the field. Exhausted we gain the forest and are finally able to stand up. Quietly we move towards the amphitheatre where we find the rest of the group.

We move deeper into the forest to wait for daybreak. The projection needs to work in full daylight since the image involves bending light and using the light to bring the vision contained in the image. We wait until the morning,

But to our disappointment the sky is cloudy. We need full sunlight to project the image. We wait and hope. We move back into the forest and continue waiting. Will the clouds break up? We might have to wait for another day.

Chapter Thirty

Sometime in the afternoon we see an opening in the clouds and a burst of sunlight. If the opening allows the sun to shine through we can create the image against a background of clouds. It will be effective. We wait, but just as the sun begins to shine through the clouds a consort of helicopters approaches the amphitheatre. They circle and move away. We wait. With the sun coming through the conditions are ideal. We move into the amphitheatre hoping we can project before we are discovered.

The watchers enter first and the rest of us follow sitting silently and facing the city. We have spent hours concentrating on the images in preparation. We see a thin haze begin to form between the city and the clouds. As more of us join in the visualization the haze thickens into a dense mist. A brilliant light radiates from the highest layer bathing all of us in its golden hues.

The mist takes on the same golden color. And within the mist we see other colors and shapes form and begin vibrating. In rhythm with the vibration we hear a strange unearthly music. We have built a passage into the other world and we are able to see clearly what our world will become. We have created an image of the indescribable beauty that flows from Being, and is the source of the beauty of pure existence. Within this beauty we feel the limitless love of Being.

As the shapes form and shift, we hear the helicopters approach. We keep projecting hoping we can hold the image over the city long enough to affect the people before we are fired upon. If we can hold the vision long enough we know it will change the world. Even if we are fired upon and die we will stay and visualize the projection as long as we can.

The image remains shifting and moving across the sky. It drops down to our level enveloping us in its golden mist. It surrounds the copters as they continue firing and the bullets march towards us. At the last moment suddenly the copters climb into the sky. We don't understand. Why did they stop firing? They come towards us and we lift our eyes to the sky above. They are so close we can see their faces. They wave and smile. We see joy and love flow from them. They dip towards us and then fly off into the distance. The vision has worked.

But what about the city? Have enough people seen the image? Have they been able or willing to leave their shelters and look up to see the projection?

The loud speakers blast their message. "This is the work of the great Satan. He has sent his demonic images to tempt you. Beware or the wrath of our God will fall on you," blare the speakers. "Do not go into the streets do not look into the sky or you will be possessed." This has just the opposite effect. There has been enough preparation on our part. The people are curious. They move into the street in droves searching the skies and when they see the image, the vision, a collective sigh sounds throughout the city. The people manning the speakers are also affected and instinctively recognize the fulfillment of their deepest yearning. They recognize their truest selves and their infinite potential. Their consciousness shifts. They stop broadcasting. And then they hear the music, the music carrying traces from the source of existence, of Being, the music that drew us out of being and began our journey through all of the universes into this universe; the music that began our journey into this world. The music floats through the mist descending from the clouds and surrounds them. It sounds throughout the city and the people begin swaying and then dancing, a dance of joy and love, the dance of being and consciousness, of awareness of their divine selves.

The Holy Enforcer tries to take command. He orders his troops into the streets believing the shields on their helmets will block out the images in the sky. He marches them down the steps of the citadel and orders them to fire on the throngs of dancing, joyous people. "Dancing is banned, singing is banned, fire on them," he orders. They move closer to the crowd leveling their weapons. The music increases in sound and intensity. The vision with its golden light sinks closer to the ground until it immerses them.

The crowds do not disperse but move towards the soldiers and instead of attacking them the people tear off their helmets and shields. The soldiers throw down their weapons and look up into the sky. More soldiers begin tearing off their helmets and the helmets of their fellow soldiers and point up into the sky. They look, and begin to weep. They begin weeping tears of sadness for what they have done and then they begin to weep tears of joy as they find true freedom. They join the dancing crowd.

The Holy Enforcer surrounded by his commanders, orders them to begin firing on the troops, firing into the crowd. But they refuse. Screaming he pulls out his pistol and threatens them. They quickly disarm him and pull him into the ruling room, where they leave him in isolation. He continues screaming at them but they ignore him and go out into the sunlight. They no longer wish to rule- no power, no rules, and, no bans. They sit by themselves on the steps of the citadel watching the crowd and then one by one begin to leave. Looking into the sky they too begin to weep.

We come down from the hills arm in arm dancing and singing. The vision remains in the sky and we realize the people in the city are now adding to the projection. They want it to last. Each one contributes their distinctive tone to the depth and color of the image. They want to be part of the creation of this new world. Lucia and I remain in each other's arms laughing and rejoicing. The long winter of repression is over. People are free to love, dance, create and build a new society based on love and caring. It is the new time.

Stirring

In silence – from silence
In darkness – from darkness
Song comes.
Unheard, unseen, unfelt
Dreammind, dreambody
Membrance below sound,
Membrance below sight,
Membrance below touch,
Membrance below thought.

Out of the all
The stirring begins.
Out of endless light (or love)
The stretching begins.
Through all unseen places
The seeking begins.
Wanting closeness, touching.
ending begins,
And in their end
Is our beginning.

About the author

D r. Biagi is an accomplished painter, poet and physicist. His most recent book is *The Woman Out of the Now,* a metaphysical fantasy in which he describes the power of art to bring about an evolution of consciousness and the transformations of society.

He has a doctorate in physics from the University of Colorado, a post-baccalaureate certificate in fine arts from the Maryland Institute College Arts and studied the humanities at New York University. He was a member of the theater group Theater Lab West and directed a project supported by the National Endowment for the Arts. He brings these interests to this novel combining contemporary physics, cosmology, art and spirituality.

He is also the author of a collection of paintings and poems in which the union of images and words re-creates our origin at the core of the universe and our journey into this world.

Dr. Biagi resides in Santa Fe, New Mexico where his art is represented by the gallery, Vivo Contemporary and where he practices the movement art, **NIA.**